BRING IT!

BRING IT!

Adapted by N.B. Grace

Based on the series created by Chris Thompson

Part One is based on the episode, "Give It Up," written by Rob Lotterstein

Part Two is based on the episode, "Glitz It Up," written by John D. Beck & Ron Hart

Disney • PRESS
NEW YORK

DANCE IT UP

Printed in the United States of America

First Edition
1 3 5 7 9 10 8 6 4 2
J689-1817-1-12167

ISBN 978-1-4231-6336-7

For more Disney Press fun, visit www.disneybooks.com
Visit DisneyChannel.com

PART ONE

CHAPTER 1

THE SET OF *Shake It Up, Chicago* was in full swing, and, as usual, host Gary Wilde was fired up. He stood on the metal riser above the stage, faced the camera, and said into his microphone: "And now, *Shake It Up, Chicago* presents the spotlight dance of the week. Let's hear it for the one, the only, CeCe Jones!"

The lights hit the back of the stage. The audience could see a silhouette of CeCe

1

striking a pose. Then the backdrop parted and she strutted out onto the stage, wearing a shiny gold dress, matching knee-high boots, silver tights, and a gold bow in her long auburn hair. She sparkled under the stage lights as she began to dance.

She wowed the crowd with her fancy moves, and the audience went wild! The soundstage was filled with the sounds of people cheering and applauding—and CeCe loved it!

She smiled as she pulled off a few of her really sophisticated moves. This was the spot-light dance, which meant she was right where she belonged—in the spotlight!

Suddenly, her best friend, Rocky Blue, walked out on the stage with a quizzical look on her face. Unlike CeCe, Rocky was not dressed for a performance. This was unusual because both CeCe and Rocky wanted to be professional dancers. As two of the teen dancers on the

TV dance show *Shake It Up, Chicago*, they were already well on their way to success.

But now, in spite of the fact that the music was pumping and the stage lights were shining, Rocky was wearing a very ordinary outfit—a pink sweater, short plaid skirt, and ankle boots with gray socks. She certainly wasn't dressed for the spotlight dance!

CeCe started to push her friend aside. "Hit the road," she told Rocky. "This is a solo gig."

Rocky sighed. "CeCe, you're asleep. This is a dream," she said.

"I know," CeCe grinned. "A dream come *true!*"

Rocky shook her head, her dark curls cascading around her shoulders. "You don't find it strange that you were making out with Robert Pattinson before you came out here and started dancing?"

CeCe cast her eyes to the ceiling—as if it was odd that she had been kissing the handsome star of the most popular vampire movie ever!

"Don't worry, I didn't let him bite my neck," CeCe replied.

"Okay, if this isn't a dream, then why is Gary Wilde dressed as a giant hot dog, dancing with some mustard?" Rocky asked, pointing offstage.

CeCe looked at where her friend was pointing. Sure enough, the host of the show was dressed in a hot-dog costume. And, he was dancing with someone wearing a costume that looked like a jar of mustard! CeCe's face fell. *Was* this all a dream?

Still asleep in her bed, CeCe pulled her comforter tighter around her. "I'm a star. No, I'm a superstar. I'm a star," she said, muttering to herself.

"Wake up," Rocky said softly, giving her a gentle nudge.

CeCe slept on.

Rocky tried again. "Wake up," she murmured.

CeCe snuggled deeper into her bed.

"Wake up!" Rocky yelled.

"Aah!" CeCe jerked awake. "Oh, hey, Rocky. I was having a dream and you were there, and Gary Wilde was a hot dog dancing with some mustard. What do you think that's about?"

Rocky chuckled and rolled her eyes. "Um, that you shouldn't have eaten four hot dogs last night."

"Wow," CeCe said, impressed. "You're good."

Rocky brushed off CeCe's last comment. It was time to get down to business. "Okay, get up, get dressed. You know Mrs. Locassio from the third floor?"

"The woman who doesn't like you?"

Rocky frowned. "She *does* like me," she insisted. "*Everyone* likes me! Anyway, I volunteered us at her senior center, and we're going to perform for them this morning."

This news made CeCe clutch her pillow tightly. "Senior center? Unless you're talking

5

about high school seniors, I'm going back to sleep."

But Rocky was adamant. "Wake up," she insisted, grabbing a pillow and hitting CeCe with it.

"I'm up, I'm up, I'm up!" CeCe exclaimed. It looked like her best friend simply wasn't going to take no for an answer. Like it or not, she had some volunteering to do!

CHAPTER 2

A SHORT TIME LATER, CeCe and Rocky were performing one of their favorite dance routines in the community room at the senior center. The music was blasting as they moved and grooved. The members of the senior center were nodding to the beat; some were even tapping their toes. Everyone seemed to be having a good time.

"Isn't community service great?" Rocky asked, smiling at their audience.

"Sure, if you're trying to stay out of jail," CeCe said, although she was smiling, too. Dancing for an audience always put her in a good mood.

"Whoo!" CeCe cheered as she and Rocky coordinated their moves for a big finish.

Only one person didn't seem to be enjoying herself. A white-haired woman wearing a red tracksuit sat on the couch, scowling at CeCe and Rocky.

When the music ended, Rocky went over to sit next to the woman.

"What's the matter, Mrs. Locassio?" Rocky asked. "Is your arthritis acting up so you can't clap your hands?"

"You call that *dancing*?" Mrs. Locassio snapped. "I danced better than that when I was a Vegas showgirl! Of course," the older woman said, "that was before I had my hip replaced."

Rocky smiled politely. "Well, let's see how

good you really are, 'cause it's time for everyone to dance!" she said brightly.

While the music played, CeCe and Rocky encouraged the senior citizens to dance. CeCe stood behind a man who sat in a wheelchair, a brightly colored afghan over his knees, and helped him wave his hands in the air in time with the music.

"Oh, yeah!" CeCe said enthusiastically. "Say what? Say what? Who's got the groove? Who's got the groove?"

The man winced. "I don't know about the groove, but I know I got the gout," he said.

"Come on," Rocky said to Mrs. Locassio, trying to pull her to her feet. "Dancing is a great way to get some exercise and increase mobility."

"I don't want to dance," Mrs. Locassio snarled.

Rocky tugged her arm again, but Mrs. Locassio wouldn't move. "Leave me alone!" she snapped angrily.

Rocky tried again to get the woman to stand up, but she just glared at her.

"I don't like you," Mrs. Locassio said finally.

Rocky wasn't going to let that comment go by without a comeback. She put her hands on the arm of the sofa, kicked up a foot, and said, as charmingly as she could, "Well, sure you do. I mean, everybody likes me. I'm adorable."

"Come on! Dance!" CeCe ordered.

Finally, Rocky managed to pull Mrs. Locassio up off the couch. "Come on, let's have fun!" She laughed. "Ready?"

She began moving her hips from side to side. "Ooh, ooh, ooh, ooh, ooh!" she crooned to the music.

Unfortunately, Rocky went one "ooh" too far. She swung her hips a little too fast—and knocked into Mrs. Locassio!

"Ow!" she cried, glaring at Rocky. "I think you broke my *other* hip!"

"Sorry," Rocky said, biting her lip. Her campaign to get Mrs. Locassio to realize how much she liked her was definitely *not* off to a good start!

♪ ♪ ♪

It was Saturday and, as always, *Shake It Up, Chicago* was airing live. CeCe and Rocky stood with the other performers on the sidelines as a boy performed an amazing dance routine. He popped, he locked, he spun, he jumped—he was whirling around the stage like an Olympic gymnast!

As CeCe clapped along to the music, she said, "Uh-huh. Oh, yeah. Say what? Say what? Yeah!"

"Wow!" Rocky exclaimed. "This guy is amazing! I mean, does he even have bones in his body? He's like a jellyfish. A dancing jellyfish."

"I'll never get a spotlight dance," CeCe said in despair. "Why did I have to be born with a spinal column?"

The dancer grinned at the audience, pointed

his finger at them, and exited the stage.

Gary Wilde, the host of the show, bounded onstage, his microphone in hand. "That was Johnny B in the spotlight dance!" he exclaimed, grinning. Then he put on a serious expression. "Let's get real, now. Next week, *Shake It Up* presents our all-day dance marathon. We're raising money for local charities because *Shake It Up* cares."

He bowed his head—until he heard someone say, "And cut! That's a wrap."

Instantly, Gary dropped his sincere act. "Ugh, glad that's done," he said in relief, loosening his tie. "All right, listen up dancers. I need you to pick a partner and a charity for the marathon. Start signing up sponsors, people. Last couple standing wins five grand for their cause."

Rocky's eyes lit up. She turned to CeCe and said excitedly, "Whoa, that can help the senior center! We can get them a new couch, a new stereo, all the prune juice they can drink."

CeCe rolled her eyes. "Rocky, enough with the charity work already. I'm not wasting another Saturday. We're out!"

Gary turned back to add one more announcement. "And don't forget, the last couple standing also wins a special spotlight dance of the week."

CeCe felt a thrill of excitement go through her.

"We're in!" she said quickly, grabbing Rocky's hands and holding them up to show that they would be dancing as a team.

After all, charity was all well and good, but getting to do the spotlight dance—*that* was a dream come true!

CHAPTER 3

THE NEXT DAY, Rocky's older brother, Ty, and Rocky and CeCe's friend Deuce Martinez were hurrying down the school hallway between classes. Ty was carrying a clipboard with a sheet of paper.

"Okay, who's going to sponsor my sister Rocky in the *Shake It Up* marathon?" Ty asked the students scurrying past. Then he spotted someone he knew.

"Hey, Tommy," Ty said, pushing the other

student up against the lockers. He began frisking him. "Come on, people. Give till it hurts. Or at least until this sheet is filled up."

"Dude, it wouldn't kill *you* to make a donation," Deuce said.

"I am making a donation—of my time," Ty pointed out.

"Cheap," Deuce said, mimicking the chirping sound of a chicken. "Cheap-cheap-cheap-cheap-cheap."

"Get off my back, man," Ty said. "I'm saving up for a car."

"Yeah. Well, I bet it'll be a *cheap* car," Deuce taunted. "Cheap-cheap-cheap."

"Maybe it will. But I'm not giving you a ride. Walk," Ty said, adding in a high-pitched voice, "walk-walk-walk-walk-walk-walk-walk."

This argument was interrupted by the arrival of Tinka and Gunther Hessenheffer, who were exchange students at the high school and also dancers on *Shake It Up, Chicago*. They were twins, with the same blond hair, the same foreign accent, and the same snide attitude. Today they were even wearing matching denim vests trimmed with fur!

"Oh, look who's still trying to get sponsors for the marathon," Tinka said in a mocking voice.

"Our sheet's already filled up," Gunther bragged. "We stood outside our papa's butcher shop, and everyone who pledged got a free garlic sausage."

"Mmm." Gunther and Tinka both smacked their lips as if they could still taste that delicious sausage.

"Who are you guys dancing for?" Ty asked.

"Well, if you must know, we will be shaking our money makers for the *Mousse* Foundation," Gunther said.

Deuce wrinkled his forehead, puzzled. "Since when are *moose* an endangered species?"

"Not *this* moose," Tinka said, holding her hands to her head to mimic antlers. "*This* mousse." She ran her hand through Gunther's styled hair.

He grinned, then said in a serious voice, "Mousse Foundation provides hair-care products for underprivileged children."

"But not just mousse," Tinka added in a more upbeat voice. "Also gels, shampoos, and conditioners."

"Thanks to the Mousse Foundation, the less fortunate never looked more fabulous!" Gunther finished, spreading his arms in a "ta-da!" gesture.

Tinka smirked at Deuce and then ruffled his hair. "You could use a little help," she told him.

Ty couldn't help laughing and pointing at Deuce. Tinka was annoying, but that *was* funny!

CHAPTER 4

CECE AND ROCKY had raced to the senior center to tell them the good news about the dance marathon.

"And the last couple standing wins five grand for their charity!" Rocky wrapped up their presentation with enthusiasm.

Most of the members of the senior center clapped and smiled at this.

One person, of course, did not.

"You two will never win the marathon," said Mrs. Locassio sourly from her seat at a bingo table. "You're too weak and scrawny. What we need are a couple of fat broads dancing for us."

A couple of men nodded to each other at this. Dancing a marathon took a lot of stamina. Maybe the girls wouldn't be up to it. . . .

"Come on, Mrs. Locassio," Rocky pleaded. "Everybody else seems to be excited about this."

"You think they're excited now?" she scoffed. "Watch this. Bingo!"

The players at the other tables smiled and clapped.

Rocky and CeCe realized that Mrs. Locassio was right—people *were* just as excited about someone getting bingo as they were about the dance marathon!

CeCe pulled Rocky to one side.

"Would it kill her to say thank you?" CeCe muttered.

"CeCe, this isn't about getting props, it's about bringing a little joy to the elderly," Rocky said. "Besides, Mrs. Locassio reminds me of my grandmother."

She gave the older woman a kind smile. Mrs. Locassio simply made a face at her in return.

"Really?" CeCe asked, trying to sound innocent. "Your grandmother doesn't like you?"

Rocky's smile vanished. "Grammy likes me! Mrs. Locassio likes me! *Everyone* likes me!"

She took a deep breath, realizing that she was yelling, and then forced a sweet smile on her face. She walked back to the table where Mrs. Locassio was sitting. "I love your macaroni sculpture," she cooed, looking at the artwork. "You're a very talented artist."

"Let me know when you stop talking," Mrs. Locassio grumbled. "I'll turn my hearing aid back on."

Rocky's face fell, and CeCe gasped. No one

could speak to her best friend that way—not even a senior citizen!

"Well, before you do, I have a few choice words for you—" CeCe began hotly.

Quickly, Rocky clapped a hand over CeCe's mouth and dragged her away.

Getting Mrs. Locassio to admit she liked her was already an uphill battle. . . . If she let CeCe keep talking, she might as well give up now!

♪ ♪ ♪

A few days later, Rocky paid CeCe a visit at home. "Hey, hey, hey!" Rocky said cheerfully as she climbed through the window of the Joneses' apartment from the fire escape outside.

"Yo, Rocky," CeCe said.

Rocky took a seat at the kitchen counter.

"Look what I got us for the *Shake It Up* marathon," CeCe said, handing Rocky a can. "Bang Pow Zoom energy drink."

Rocky took a closer look at the label and frowned. "Wait. Each can has more caffeine than three cups of coffee."

"Exactly." CeCe nodded. "But you're saying it all wrong." She held a can up next to her face and gave a big smile, as if she were in a commercial. Then, in an upbeat, enthusiastic tone, she said, "Each can has more caffeine than three cups of coffee!"

"If we drink all this, we'll be up till Christmas," Rocky said.

"Exactly," CeCe said. "But you're saying it all wrong." She put on her TV-commercial expression and said brightly, "If we drink this—"

Rocky put her hand over CeCe's mouth. She had learned from experience this was the best—if not the only—way to get her friend to be quiet!

"Yeah, yeah, I get it," Rocky said as they both sat down on the couch. "But drinking this is like a professional athlete taking steroids before a game."

CeCe opened her eyes wide. "What? It's just fruit punch with a little kick!"

Rocky shook her head slowly. "That's how it starts. First, energy drinks. Then that leads to harder stuff." She started talking faster and louder, hoping to convince CeCe. "Next thing you know, you're thrown off the show, you drop out of school, your mom kicks you out, and then you're living behind a Dumpster."

CeCe stared at her friend. "Fine," she said. "But if we don't get that spotlight dance—"

Rocky shot her a sharp look.

CeCe caught herself. "I mean, money for those sweet senior citizens," she said smoothly.

As the girls left the apartment to go sit on the stoop in front of their building, CeCe called over her shoulder, "Be back soon."

They had barely left when Flynn, CeCe's younger brother, came into the living room in search of his baseball glove.

He spotted it on the end table and picked it up. Then he noticed something even more interesting—the energy drink that CeCe and Rocky had left on the coffee table.

"Bang Pow Zoom?" he said aloud. He had never heard of this drink before, but it had a great name. It sounded like something a superhero would drink!

He popped the can open and took a gulp.

Within seconds, his eyes lit up and his whole body shuddered.

"Me likey!" he shouted.

CHAPTER 5

ROCKY AND CECE were hanging out on the steps in front of CeCe's apartment building when Deuce walked up the street.

"Girls!" he called out.

"Hey, Deuce," CeCe said.

He held up a few articles of clothing. "Look, my cousin Sarafina is launching a line of really cool clothes, and I'm doing a little market research for her. What do you think?"

CeCe's and Rocky's eyes lit up. "Ooh," they both said.

"Hang on." Deuce pushed a button on a pair of pants. Instantly, lights started flashing on the pant legs!

"Ah!" CeCe and Rocky said, even more impressed.

"Nice couture, huh?" Deuce asked. "Sarafina told me 'couture' means 'fancy clothes,'" he admitted. "You like?"

CeCe sighed. "No," she said. "We *love!*"

He handed the clothes to Rocky. "Good, 'cause they're yours."

"Thanks, Deuce!" CeCe exclaimed. "You're the best!"

Rocky looked at him curiously. "Yeah, but what's the catch?"

Deuce looked insulted. "Why do you always think I'm working some angle?" he asked. He looked at the girls and put on a sad expression.

Both girls raised their eyebrows at that. They knew him way too well.

He shrugged. "Okay, so here's the angle," he began. "You have to wear it in the marathon and give her a little free advertising."

CeCe grinned as she reached for the clothes. "No problem!"

Rocky pulled the clothes away from her. "Yes, *problem*! It seems selfish to use a charity event to promote somebody's business. We're supposed to be dancing to help old people."

"Cousin Sarafina *is* old," Deuce protested. "She's twenty-six!"

Rocky hesitated. The clothes *were* super cute. . . . "Well, charity does begin at home," she said, weakening.

CeCe laughed as they grabbed the clothes. They were both going to look awesome in their electric pants! No one else would stand a chance next to them!

♪ ♪ ♪

A few moments later, Rocky and CeCe went back inside and headed to CeCe's apartment.

Once in the apartment, CeCe stopped and frowned. She had just spotted three empty cans on the table. "What happened to all the energy drinks?"

Flynn ran into the living room and raced around the table a few times, shouting, "Bang! Pow! Zoom!"

CeCe's eyes opened wide. "Oh, Rocky, get him!" she yelled. "Get him!"

The girls chased Flynn, but he was really fast!

"I'll get him, too," Rocky said, grabbing Flynn by the shoulders as CeCe grabbed his feet.

"You know what creeps me out? Tuna," Flynn babbled. "Packed in water or packed in oil. Make a decision!"

The girls tossed him on the couch.

"You know what else creeps me out?" Flynn went on, talking even faster. "The vowels. I get A, E, I, O, and U, but why Y? Why Y?"

Rocky looked down at Flynn and sighed. "It's going to be a long night," she predicted.

CHAPTER 6

EARLY THE NEXT MORNING, Rocky and CeCe staggered into CeCe's bedroom. Their eyes were half-shut, their hair was tangled, and they could hardly stand up.

"*So* tired," Rocky said, collapsing onto CeCe's bed.

"Must sleep," CeCe said, falling onto the mattress next to her.

They were both about to drift off to sleep

when the laptop next to the bed suddenly began sounding an alarm. The words "Dance Marathon Today!" blinked on the laptop's screen.

"Eight a.m.?" Rocky asked in disbelief.

"I just had the worst dream," CeCe groaned. "We were supposed to dance all day long in the marathon, but Flynn kept us up the entire night before."

Flynn's head popped up from under the covers.

"Could you keep it down?" he demanded. "I'm trying to sleep!"

♪ ♪ ♪

CeCe and Rocky would have loved nothing more than going to sleep themselves—preferably for many hours. But they had made a promise to dance in the marathon, and they knew that professional dancers always showed up for gigs.

Still, it was hard to stay awake at the makeup table. Both CeCe and Rocky were nodding off when Deuce sauntered into the studio and spotted them.

"Ladies! You're looking—" he greeted them with a big smile, which instantly faded. "I was going to say 'good,' but now I'm going to go with 'yuck.'"

CeCe and Rocky looked in the mirror. They gasped.

Rocky's eye shadow was smeared, and CeCe had completely missed her mouth when putting on her lipstick—in fact, she had a streak of bright red across her cheek!

"He's right," Rocky said. "We look terrible."

Gary strode out from backstage, dressed in a gray suit, dark gray shirt, and white bow tie. The dancers, including Gunther and Tinka, quickly gathered around the host.

"Okay, everyone, quick reminder," Gary said. "No matter what, don't stop moving on the dance floor or you're out! Now, we're about to go live on the air. So, what happens here will be broadcast out there, as it happens. Now remember, kids, there's a lot riding on this marathon."

"Yeah," CeCe said wistfully. "The spotlight dance."

"He meant a lot of money for charity," Rocky corrected her. "Can't you not think about yourself for, like, one minute?"

"You're right," CeCe said sarcastically. "I'll just think about Mrs. Locassio and how she doesn't like you."

"She *does* like me," Rocky insisted. "*Everybody* likes me!"

Unfortunately, she said this within earshot of Gunther and Tinka, their biggest dance rivals. Rocky sighed. She was sure they'd make some sort of snide comment.

"Not *everybody*," Tinka replied with a mean smile.

Rocky shot her a look, but there wasn't time to get into an argument. The cameras had started to roll!

Gary stood on the stage, looked into the camera lens, and said, "Welcome to the *Shake It Up* charity dance marathon. I'm Gary Wilde! The pledge lines are now open, and it's time to get the party started!"

He was so excited, he actually did a high kick! The marathon was officially underway!

The dancers hit the stage and started dancing.

CeCe and Rocky smiled at each other. Sure, they felt a little tired, but here they were, doing what they had always dreamed of—dancing on live TV! They had to keep going, no matter what, in order to win that money for the senior center.

And to do the spotlight dance, of course . . .

♪ ♪ ♪

Back in the Joneses' apartment, Ty was babysitting Flynn and tuning in to the marathon, which he was watching on his laptop at the kitchen counter.

"I swear, I'm never touching another energy

drink as long as I live," Flynn said, slapping himself on the face.

"Good," Ty said. "Because the less energy you have, the easier you are to babysit."

Flynn plopped down on the couch. "I would object to being called a baby, but right now I need a nap," Flynn yawned. "I'm so tired."

He spotted a can of energy drink on the table. "You know, I could really go for a few sips of—" Almost without meaning to, he began to reach for it.

And, just in time, he realized what he was about to do!

"What am I saying?" He grabbed the hand that was reaching for the drink and pulled it back. "Must stay away from that devil juice."

"Yo," Ty said. "Check this out."

He carried the laptop over to the couch so Flynn could see the screen.

Gary was addressing the camera from a metal

catwalk that had been erected over the stage. Three people were sitting next to him, answering phones and taking pledges.

"It's been three hours and we're still shaking it up for charity," Gary said. "Call that number on your screen or text a pledge to six-seven-six-seven."

One of the pledge takers handed him a slip of paper.

Gary read it quickly and then said, "Oh. Look here, folks. We've got a challenge! Deuce has donated five dollars and is challenging Ty Blue to meet it or beat it."

Surprised, Ty leaned in closer to look at the screen. "What?"

"And he also wants me to add this," Gary said in a high-pitched voice: "Cheap, cheap, cheap, cheap, cheap, cheap, cheap!"

Ty's mouth dropped open in shock. "He's calling me out? Deuce is calling me out? What does he think, I'm his little puppet? He pulls the strings, and I pick up the phone and make a donation?" he scoffed.

Then he felt a surge of competitive spirit. If Deuce thought he was going to show Ty up on live TV, he had another thing coming!

Ty turned to Flynn. "What was that number again?"

CHAPTER 7

BACK AT THE *Shake It Up* studio, the dancers were clearly showing the strain of dancing for hours. Rocky and CeCe were yawning as they danced. Two other competitors collapsed on the stage and instantly fell asleep.

"Another one bites the dust!" Gary cried. "Well, who could be at the top of their game after four grueling hours?"

He thought about that for a second and then

grinned. "Oh, that's right. Me, Gary Wilde. Oh, thank you!"

One of the pledge takers handed him a piece of paper with the details of a new pledge.

"Oh, here's a generous donation from Ty Blue, pledging twenty dollars in support of his sister, Rocky," Gary said.

When CeCe and Rocky heard this, they waved excitedly at the camera to thank Ty.

Gary went on reading. "The pledge is also in memory of his friend Deuce, who is now dead to him," he added, frowning.

Back in the living room, Ty laughed. "Ha! Take that, Deuce. And it only cost me twenty bucks."

From his spot on the couch, Flynn managed to summon enough energy to set Ty straight. "No, it costs you twenty bucks for every hour they dance. Even I know that, and I'm eight."

"But they've already been dancing for four

hours!" Ty said, shocked. "That's . . . That's, um . . ."

He stared into space, trying to do the math in his head.

"Eighty bucks, genius," Flynn said, rolling his eyes.

"I have to get down to the studio and stop them from dancing," Ty said. "I need to fix this!"

"And I need to nap," Flynn said.

Ty picked up Flynn and threw him over his shoulder. "You'll just have to nap up here," he said.

"This is outrageous!" Flynn protested. "Just wait till my mom hears about—"

But he was too tired to go on. He began snoring as Ty headed out the door to the studio.

♫ ♫ ♫

Flynn wasn't the only person who was tired. CeCe and Rocky could barely move around the stage!

And they weren't alone. The other dancers were doing their best just to stay upright.

Gary prowled across the stage, watching the dancers closely to see which ones were dancing—and which ones were simply asleep on their feet.

As he passed CeCe and Rocky, he gave them a sharp look. They immediately straightened up and tried to look energetic.

"Oh, yeah!" they cried as they danced faster.

"Whoo!" Rocky added for good measure.

Gary nodded, satisfied, and walked on. He stopped in front of one couple who were standing still and leaning on each other, their eyes closed.

He waved a hand in front of their faces and got no reaction.

Then he snapped his fingers—and they fell to the floor, fast asleep!

As production assistants rushed over to help

the fallen dancers to their feet, Gary walked to the nearest camera.

"We're going to give our four remaining couples a little break and go to a commercial," Gary said. "We'll be right back." He pointed at the camera and spoke to the audience. "You better be, too!"

All the dancers dropped to the floor, taking advantage of the chance to rest.

All the dancers, that is, except Tinka and Gunther. They kept grooving on the stage.

"You guys *do* know that you don't have to dance during the break, right?" CeCe asked.

"We know," Gunther said brightly. "We are just rubbing ourselves in your face!"

Tinka laughed. "Ready, Gunther?" she asked. When he nodded, she said, "Let's freak."

The brother and sister suddenly began shaking as if they had been hit by a volt of electricity!

"And again," Gunther said.

She nodded eagerly and they started shaking again, this time even faster.

CeCe and Rocky were too exhausted to even roll their eyes at this. They walked offstage just as Ty entered the studio, still carrying Flynn over his shoulder. He put the young boy on the floor, where he could sleep among the dancers taking naps.

Ty walked over to where CeCe and Rocky were sitting in front of the makeup mirrors. They were both nodding off.

"Wow, you two look sleepy," he said happily. "And you're getting sleepier." He began to sing. "Lullaby and good night. La la la–"

Rocky lifted her head and blinked at him sleepily. "What are you doing?"

"Cheering you on," Ty said.

CeCe gave him a skeptical look. "Really?" she asked. "Because it sounds more like you're putting us to sleep."

Ty did his best to laugh this off. "Don't be ridiculous!" Then he began to sing again. "Lullaby and good night. La—"

The girls started to drift off again.

Ty felt a moment of hope. Maybe they would sleep right through the break! Maybe they wouldn't be able to keep on dancing! Maybe he wouldn't have to pay any more money—

Just then, Deuce rushed up to him. He grabbed Ty's jacket and pulled him away from the girls.

"Ladies, you're doing great," Deuce said loudly, waking up CeCe and Rocky. "Don't forget to show the Sarafina label every chance you get and keep the lights on."

He pushed a button on CeCe's pants to make them light up.

But even this wasn't enough to encourage CeCe.

Yawning, she said, "I don't know how much longer I can do this. I'm running on fumes."

"You just need a jump start," Deuce said. He pinched her arm.

"Ow!" CeCe glared at him. She was definitely awake now—*and* mad. "You-you just pinched me. What was that for?"

Deuce put on a very earnest expression. "I did it for the old people."

♪ ♪ ♪

Some time later, the marathon was still going on, although the energy level was definitely lower. Even Gary had untied his tie and unbuttoned the top button of his shirt, although he still looked fresher than any of the dancers.

"As we enter our eighth hour, we go remote to one of the charities our finalists are competing for," he said into his microphone. "Welcome to *Shake It Up Cares*."

The camera switched to the senior center. It showed Mrs. Locassio sitting on the couch.

"It's a pleasure to be here. I've never seen your show before," she said, smiling. Then her smile turned to a scowl. "It's awful!"

Gary chuckled. "Aren't the elderly adorable? Anyway, Rocky and CeCe are dancing their little butts off for you. Is there something you'd like to say to them?"

"Yes, there is," Mrs. Locassio said. Then she told Gary that CeCe was a bad dancer!

CeCe gasped and stopped dancing for a moment. She had a lot of confidence as a performer, but a comment like that would make anyone angry!

But Mrs. Locassio wasn't done. "And tell the big one I have cataracts, but even *I* can see she has a zit on her forehead."

Mortified, Rocky put a hand up to cover her face.

"That's it," CeCe said angrily. "I don't have to take that from some old, cranky neighbor lady. I'm out."

She headed for the side of the stage.

Rocky followed her. "We have to be the last ones standing," she said.

CeCe turned to face Rocky and moved her feet, just enough to keep from being disqualified. She was ready to quit—more than ready!—but she wanted to hear what her friend had to say first.

"Why bother to dance for someone who doesn't even appreciate it?" CeCe demanded.

Rocky was too tired and angry to pretend any more. "'Cause I am going to get a thank you from that old bat if it kills me!" she shouted, exasperated.

CeCe's eyes brightened. At last, Rocky was telling the truth. "Aha!" she cried.

"Aha, *what*?" Rocky said uncomfortably.

"Aha, I was right," CeCe said. "This is all about Mrs. Locassio!"

"Fine," Rocky said. "I admit it. But I don't care. I'm going to get her to like me."

"Rocky, why does everyone have to like you?" CeCe asked, genuinely puzzled.

"Because when people like you, it means you're a good person," Rocky answered. She looked really worried that she might not live up to this standard.

CeCe couldn't believe it! How could Rocky think she wasn't a good person, even for a second? She always had a cause to promote, a person to help, an idea for making the world better . . .

CeCe put a hand on her friend's arm. "Rocky, trust me," she said, looking directly at her. "You're the best person I know."

Rocky smiled at her shyly. "Hearing that from you is even better than hearing it from Mrs. Locassio."

CeCe's face filled with hope. "So we can stop dancing now?" she asked eagerly.

But Rocky shook her head. Her smiled turned into a look of grim determination. "No way," she said firmly. "We're going to be the last ones standing, even if you're *not* standing."

She grabbed CeCe's arms and pulled them over her shoulder, than began moving around the dance floor, dragging CeCe with her.

On the other side of the stage, Tinka and Gunther were yawning.

"I am all pooped out," Tinka said. "I give up."

"What if Poppa gave up when he was carrying you across the mountain to freedom?" Gunther asked.

"What are you talking about?" Tinka asked, puzzled. "We flew here. Business class."

Gunther sighed. It was hard to give a pep talk to someone who always took things so literally! As he was trying to come up with a way to convince his sister to keep dancing, another couple collapsed.

That left Gunther and Tinka facing off against Rocky and CeCe.

"And we're down to our final two couples," Gary said gleefully. "How much longer can they last?"

It was a good question—but not one that Flynn was interested in. He yawned loudly. Then, he spotted a can of energy drink on one of the dressing tables.

"Bang Pow Zoom," he said happily. "Hello, old friend."

While he was sneaking away with the can, Rocky and CeCe had finally hit the wall.

"I don't think I can carry you anymore," Rocky said. "I mean, we did our best, and we said we would dance till we dropped."

"And now it's time to drop," CeCe agreed. It was too bad they couldn't keep going, but enough was enough. She hugged Rocky. "Sorry."

Rocky smiled and hugged CeCe back . . . then she jumped away from her, her eyes wide.

"Ow!" Rocky cried. "My pants just shocked me!"

CeCe jerked as her vest lit up.

"Ow! My top zapped *me*!" CeCe shouted.

Ty couldn't help grinning as he watched CeCe and Rocky staggering about the stage, jerking each time they were shocked.

"I don't think your cousin Sarafina is going to be on *Project Runway* any time soon," he said to Deuce.

"Well, she can't go back to being an electrician," Deuce said. "She was lousy at that."

Just then, Gunther and Tinka collapsed to the floor.

"And the official winners of the marathon are Rocky and CeCe!" Gary announced. "As the last standing couple, they will now close our show with the spotlight dance of the week! Take it away, girls!"

But CeCe and Rocky had had enough. When the camera turned to them, the audience did not see them performing a spotlight dance.

Instead, they were fast asleep on the floor!

Gary looked from them to the camera, his mouth hanging open in dismay. How could they finish the show if they didn't have marathon winners performing a spotlight dance? He shook his head in disappointment. He couldn't believe the girls had blown their chance for a spotlight dance!

Luckily, there was still some entertainment to be had. Hyped up on the energy drink, Flynn came running onto the stage.

"Yeah!" he cried as he began doing his very own, very free form, very Flynn dance. "Watch this!" he shouted.

He did a few hopscotch moves, then dropped

to the floor to spin on his back. He finished his dance by cocking his hand like a pistol and blowing on it.

"Bang! Pow! Zoom!" he said, right into the camera.

Then he, too, dropped to the floor and instantly fell into a deep, exhausted sleep.

CHAPTER 8

"**HOW ARE YOU FEELING,** little man?" Ty asked as he carried Flynn through the door of his apartment.

Unfortunately, Ty wasn't being careful, as usual. Flynn's head hit the doorjamb and Flynn grunted in pain.

"Oh, sorry," Ty said.

"I feel horrible," Flynn groaned. "I've got a headache, and I'm exhausted."

Ty shook his head. "Those energy drinks are bad for kids." He carefully put Flynn down in a comfortable chair.

"Never again," Flynn said in heartfelt tones. "Thanks for taking care of me, though, Ty."

Ty sat on the coffee table and grinned at Flynn.

"No problem," he said, biting his lip. "You're just lucky you have a friend as good as me to watch your back."

Flynn didn't know it yet, but Ty had had a little fun while Flynn was sacked out.

"I [heart] Ty," was written across Flynn's forehead. A small mustache and goatee had also been drawn on his face in black paint, and he now sported long sideburns as well!

"I owe you one, buddy," Flynn said.

Ty just shook his head. "Nah," he said. "We're even."

Then he couldn't help himself. He burst out laughing.

PART TWO

CeCe rocked the *Shake It Up, Chicago* stage, even if it *was* only in a dream!

Rocky wanted to win the dance marathon so she could give the prize money to the senior center.

"Thanks to the Mousse Foundation, the less fortunate *never* looked more fabulous!" Gunther exclaimed.

Deuce convinced CeCe and Rocky to wear the flashy
couture pants for the marathon.

CeCe was so tired, she had a little trouble putting on
her makeup!

Ty couldn't afford to let Rocky and CeCe win the marathon. *Literally.*

Rocky and CeCe celebrated by taking a nap–right on the dance floor! Flynn joined them.

CeCe and Rocky were living their dream by dancing on live TV!

CeCe knew Gary Wilde, the host of *Shake it Up, Chicago,* must want *something*. He was being way too nice!

"Are you kidding me? It's like trying to eat my pillow,"
Deuce told his friend Dina, as he bit into a giant burrito.

"Besides my precious Dina, my most favorite thing on
Earth is my little piggy," Dina's dad warned Deuce.

At the Little Cutie Queen pageant, Rocky met a little girl named Eileen.

"Me and the other girls can't stand Eileen! We want your help to get her out of the contest," Sally said.

CeCe showed off her beauty-queen smile—she'd been perfecting it for years!

"There. You're perfect," CeCe said happily. "I know you're going to be the winner."

CHAPTER 1

ANOTHER HIGH-ENERGY *Shake It Up, Chicago* show was coming to an end. Half a dozen young dancers were performing—and right at the center were CeCe Jones and Rocky Blue. The two best friends wore matching hot pink *Shake It Up* jackets and ear-to-ear smiles. After all, here they were, living their dream by dancing on live TV. Life couldn't get any better than this!

Gary Wilde, the show's host, bounded onto

the set, microphone in hand. He stared into the camera and said, "See you next week for more great dancing, more great music, and more great hosting from me, Gary Wilde, on . . . *Shake It Up, Chicago!*"

The dancers all cheered and clapped energetically.

Then the cameras were turned off, and Gary turned to CeCe and Rocky.

"Hey, you two, terrific show today!" he said cheerfully. "Really, one of your best."

Rocky gave him a skeptical look. "What do you want?"

He gave her an innocent look in return. "What do you mean?"

"You only compliment us when you want us to do some funky job," CeCe said.

"Yeah, the last time you said something nice, we had to crawl into your air-conditioning vent," Rocky said, wrinkling her nose at the memory.

"I bet some of them can't even afford the good fake nails," CeCe said. She put on a sad expression and, her voice trembling with emotion, added, "That breaks my heart."

"She's right," Gary said. "We all need to do a little service for the community." He gave the girls a winning smile.

Rocky wasn't buying it. She knew him too well. "Oh, come on, Gary," she told him.

He shrugged. "Well, *technically*, I need to do a little community service," he admitted. "I have nine speeding tickets. It was this or jail," he confessed.

CeCe gave Rocky a pleading look. Rocky hesitated, but she could see that her best friend really wanted the job–and she knew that Gary needed their help.

"Okay," she finally said. "Let's do it." After all, it *was* for a good cause.

"Ah, great!" Gary exclaimed. "I'll call the pageant people and let them know my two top dancers are coming over. You guys are fantastic. The best!"

Rocky gave him a knowing look. "And here it comes," she commented.

Sure enough, Gary whipped a pair of yellow plastic gloves out of his pocket. "Cell phone fell out of my pocket," he said. "Second stall on the left."

"Whoo," Rocky and CeCe grimaced, but they took the gloves and headed for the bathroom. Dancing on a hit show certainly seemed to have a price!

♪♪♪

A short time later, as Rocky and CeCe walked through the halls of John Hughes High School, Rocky was having second thoughts about the Little Cutie Queen pageant.

"CeCe, I've been thinking and I'm not really

comfortable with beauty pageants," Rocky said. "They're demeaning to women and an archaic form of worshipping beauty over the intellectual mind."

CeCe rolled her eyes as she opened her locker and put her books away. "Can you say that again in American?" she asked.

Rocky tried again. "They teach girls that being pretty is more important than being smart," she said.

"Yeah, but they *also* teach a lot of important life lessons," CeCe countered. "Like how to put hair spray on your butt so your dress doesn't ride up!"

"Why isn't there a contest that judges young girls on how smart they are?" Rocky asked.

"There *is*," CeCe said. "It's called *school*."

Rocky couldn't really argue with that. CeCe saw that her friend was weakening and decided to push a little more.

"There was a dead-rat smell in there!" Gary protested.

"That's because there *was* a dead rat in there!" CeCe replied.

"Anyway, while I have you here . . ." Gary began.

"I knew it," Rocky said, rolling her eyes. "Gary, if your phone fell in the toilet, it is staying there."

But Gary just gave her a big smile and said, "No, no. I'm hosting Chicago's Little Cutie Queen pageant and I want you two to choreograph the show!"

All memories of dead rats and bad smells were forgotten as CeCe began jumping up and down, clapping her hands. "I want to do it! I want to do it!" she cried. "Come on, Rocky. Aren't you always trying to get me to work with disadvantaged kids?"

"How're eight-year-old beauty queens disadvantaged?" Rocky demanded.

"Come on," CeCe said, pleading. "My whole life I've wanted to be a Little Cutie Queen and win a crown. I never got to do my wave, and I was *so* good."

To demonstrate, she held up a hand and turned it back and forth in a stiff little beauty queen wave.

"You could have won Little Miss *Creepy* Queen," Rocky said.

CeCe's smile dimmed. "Cutie *Queen*," she corrected her.

"No, I meant what I said," Rocky replied as they left for their next class.

CeCe sighed. It seemed like it would take a lot of convincing to get Rocky to become a fan of beauty pageants!

CHAPTER 2

LATER THAT DAY, it was lunchtime at school. Rocky and CeCe's friend Deuce Martinez followed his friend Dina Garcia to the bench where they liked to sit and eat together.

To tell the truth, Dina was more than just a friend to Deuce–or at least he hoped she would be! She had brown curly hair, beautiful dark eyes, and enough sass to keep Deuce on his toes. In other words, she was the perfect girl for him.

Now if only he could make her see that he was the perfect boy for her! As they sat down, he cleared his throat and said, "Thanks for bringing me lunch today, Dina."

"That's okay, Deuce, my mom loves to cook," Dina said. She spoke with a thick New York accent that Deuce found adorable. She pulled a foil-wrapped item from her lunch bag. "Here's my burrito." She pulled another item from her bag. This one was five times as big! "And here's yours."

Deuce's eyes widened. "Are you kidding me? It's like trying to eat my pillow!"

"My mother says, 'A man who does not love food is a man who does not love women,'" Dina told him.

Deuce considered that for a moment. If the way to show his love was to eat a burrito that was bigger than his head—well, he was up to the challenge!

"And you only brought me one?" he asked playfully, taking a big bite. "Mmm, delicious. Is this chicken?"

"No, it's octopus," Dina said.

But even the idea of eating pieces of a rubbery, eight-armed sea creature wasn't enough to deter him.

A few moments later he decided to speak his mind. He took a deep breath. "Um. So, anyway, uh, there's something I've been meaning to talk to you about. We've been hanging out for a few weeks now—"

"And you're sick of me?" Dina interrupted. She started to stand up, looking sad. "I understand. It's happened before."

"No, no, no," Deuce said quickly. He was so eager to let her know that this was the exact opposite of what he was trying to say. "No, no, no. I totally dig you. Um, you know, instead of being Deuce and Dina"—he held out his hands to show how far apart they were—"maybe we can be, you know, 'Deuce-and-Dina.'" He clasped his hands together.

Dina's face lit up. "Are you serious?" she asked.

He grinned back. "Yeah. I even want to give you an ID bracelet." He pushed up his sleeve to show a row of silver bracelets on his arm. "Pick one. I have twenty-seven."

"Oh, baby! How sweet." Dina pushed up her own sleeve to show even more bracelets in all different colors on her arm. "I have twenty-eight. But before we can wear them, you'll need to meet my father and get his approval." She looked nervous. "And that's going to be tough. I'm Don Rio Garcia's only daughter."

"Meet your pops? Piece of cake," Deuce said confidently. "He'll love me. In case you haven't noticed, I'm kind of adorable." He gave her his cutest smile.

She chuckled. "Oh, I've noticed," Dina said.

Then her eyes narrowed as she looked past him and saw a pretty blond girl lingering in the hall and casting hopeful looks in Deuce's direction. "And it looks like Allison Kelly has noticed, too."

She raised her voice. "Keep walking, Allie!"

Allison's smile disappeared and she scurried away. After all, no one messed with Don Rio Garcia's only daughter!

CHAPTER 3

THE PAGEANT REHEARSAL room was filled with little girls wearing brightly colored dresses when CeCe and Rocky walked in. Despite the room's drab beige walls, worn beige carpet, and dim lighting, CeCe's face lit up and she looked around in wonder.

"It's just like I imagined it would be," CeCe sighed. "Isn't it magical?"

"Yeah, you can hardly tell we're in conference

room B of the Skokie Budget Inn," Rocky said sarcastically.

CeCe ignored her. She took a deep, appreciative breath. "I love the smell of rhinestones, the rustle of taffeta, the air thick with talcum powder, and the ground damp with the tears of the losers," she gushed.

Behind them, the little girls had lined up on a small stage.

Gary jumped onstage to join them. "Look, girls!" he cried, pointing at Rocky and CeCe. "They're our choreographers from *Shake It Up, Chicago!*"

The girls cheered and jumped up and down. When Rocky and CeCe went up on the stage, the Little Cutie Queen contestants gathered around them, thrilled to meet dancers they had actually seen on TV!

Gary looked at Rocky and CeCe over the little girls' heads. "Let's rehearse a segment called 'Chat with Rocky and CeCe while Gary faxes his paperwork, which proves he was here all afternoon,'" he said.

As Gary quickly left the room, CeCe and Rocky smiled at the contestants.

"Hi, girls," CeCe said. "I have an eight-year-old little brother, and I would trade him in one minute for any of you adorable little pixies."

Rocky took a deep breath. She wasn't quite as into this as CeCe was, but she was determined to do her best. As she walked past the girls, she patted each one gingerly on the head.

"Wow, that's a lot of hair," Rocky said as she touched one little girl, whose hair had been lacquered into a stylish updo. She frowned. Her fingers were now stuck on the girl's head! She pulled her hand as hard as she could to free it. "And a *lot* of hair spray!"

"Hi, sweetheart," CeCe said to a little girl with long blond curls and big blue eyes. "What's your name?"

"I'm Sally Van Buren and *Shake It Up, Chicago* is my favorite show, and *you're* my favorite dancer," the little girl said in a sugary voice as she fluttered her eyelashes. "Can I just say that you look even prettier in real life than you do on TV?"

CeCe smiled. "Not only can you say it, I'd like you to record it for my new ringtone," she said, pulling out her cell phone.

Rocky glanced past the group of girls and saw one who was standing all by herself. She wore a pretty dress like the other girls, but she had on sneakers and a baseball cap.

Rocky walked over to where the girl was leaning against the wall.

"Hey, what's your name? I'm Rocky," she said.

"I'm Eileen," she replied. "Can you do me a favor?"

"Yeah, sure, what is it?" Rocky asked, leaning down to hear what she had to say.

Eileen whispered urgently, "Get me out of here!"

Rocky straightened up again, a look of understanding on her face.

"Yeah, I'm not really that thrilled to be here either," Rocky admitted. "My best friend made me."

"Well, my mom made *me*," Eileen said, sulking. "She was a Little Cutie Queen. So were both of my sisters. And if I don't do this, she won't let me try out for the baseball team."

"You must be miserable," Rocky said sympathetically.

"Yeah, but I found something that entertains me," Eileen said with a glint of mischief. "Watch."

She turned toward the other girls and called out, "Oh, no! We're out of mascara!"

All the girls began screaming and running around in a panic. Rocky and Eileen laughed. Maybe Rocky would have a good time after all!

♪ ♪ ♪

CeCe had created what she thought was a perfect dance for the contestants to perform. It was simple enough for little girls to learn, and very charming and sweet. She stood on the stage in the *Shake It Up* studio. She thought the studio would be a good place for the girls to learn their dance routines. Or at least, she hoped it would be! She took the contestants through the steps one more time while Rocky and Gary stood on the sidelines and watched.

"Five-six-seven-eight," CeCe said, counting out each step. "One-two-three-four-five-six-seven-eight. And move and dip!"

Most of the little girls were following along just fine. Eileen, however, was having trouble.

Not only did she not have a talent for dancing, but she clearly had no interest in it. As the other girls twirled in their ruffled skirts, Eileen stomped around the stage. She had changed out of her dress and was now wearing jeans, a football jersey, and her baseball cap.

At that moment, CeCe overheard Rocky and Gary arguing and stopped the rehearsal. She headed over to them.

"Come on, Gary," Rocky was saying.

Gary shook his head, his arms crossed. "I'm not going to sing it," he insisted. "It's embarrassing."

"It's part of your community service," CeCe reminded him.

Gary sighed. Rocky had a point.

"Hit it, Marco," he said reluctantly, pointing to the sound guy.

Marco gave him a thumbs-up and started the music.

Gary walked briskly to the stage and took his spot among the Little Cutie Queen contestants.

Sheepishly, he began singing.

"In the deepest part of fairyland, where my little girl dreams come true," he warbled in a high voice. "I'll make a stop at the ice cream shop and I'll get a scoop or two. . . ."

CeCe's and Rocky's mouths dropped. Sure, Gary had said earlier the song was embarrassing, but they had never expected anything this bad!

Waving his arms in the air, Gary sidestepped across the stage.

"I'll have charm; I'll have grace," he sang. "Not a zit on my face!"

CeCe and Rocky started giggling.

Gary twirled across the stage. All the little girls twirled behind him.

He continued singing. "I'll spread my little-girl magic all over the place."

Suddenly he stopped and looked at the camera, trying to keep a straight face. "I'm a beauty queen, I'm a cutie queen, I'm a Little Cutie Queen!"

As he finished, he dropped his head in his hands, totally humiliated.

CeCe and Rocky couldn't believe it. Even though they tried very hard to contain their laughter, they just couldn't help it. They were laughing so hard their eyes were tearing! That song was one of the worst they had ever heard!

CHAPTER 4

IT WAS THE BIG DAY. Deuce was about to meet Dina's father. He was a little nervous, he had to admit—but he was also confident. After all, he *was* adorable!

Dina gave him an encouraging smile as he walked up to where her dad was sitting at a little table on the sidewalk outside an Italian bakery. Her father was dressed in a white suit with a gray vest and had a white fedora on his head.

Two large men wearing dark suits and sunglasses stood silently behind him, looking stern–and a little scary.

"Oh, hello, Mr. Garcia," Deuce said breezily. "I am Marin Martinez. But you can call me Deuce."

"I am Don Rio," Dina's father replied in a formal tone. "But you may call me Antonio Jimenez Ricardo Esteban Octavio Jose Rosario Stefan Mitch Hector Shakira Garcia."

Deuce laughed at "Shakira." Imagine, a man like Dina's father having the name of a famous Colombian singer!

"Dina didn't tell me you were funny," Deuce said, still laughing.

Don Rio gave him a cool look. "I am not. You are thinking of my brother, Juan Carlos Ernesto Pedro Paco Pancho Emiliano Zapata Jay-Z Garcia."

"Well, I'm afraid to ask what your sister's name is," Deuce said, trying to make a joke.

"Debby," Don Rio said flatly. "Deuce, please sit down."

After Deuce sat down on one of the chairs, Don Rio continued. "These are my associates, Izquierdo and Derecha. This means 'left' and 'right' in Spanish. Do I make you uncomfortable when I speak Spanish?"

"Uh, well, actually, both my parents are from Cuba—" Deuce began.

"So, you like to talk about yourself, eh, Deuce?" Don Rio interrupted.

"No, no, no," Deuce stammered. This meeting was not going well at all! "I was just saying—"

"Deuce, you remind me of myself when I was your age," said Don Rio, interrupting again. "Only I was a magnificent young soldier and you are . . ."

Deuce sat up a little straighter and gave Don Rio his best smile. But Don Rio wrinkled his nose in disgust. "All eyebrows and headphones and cheap cologne," he finished.

He turned his head to speak to his bodyguards. "Gentlemen, you know what you have to do."

One of the bodyguards nodded and reached inside his jacket.

"No!" Deuce yelled, his eyes wide. Was he going to pull out brass knuckles to hit him?

But when the bodyguard's hand appeared again, it was holding . . . a bottle of cologne.

"Cologne him!" Don Rio ordered.

The bodyguard spritzed Deuce heavily.

"How do you like it?" Dina's father asked Deuce.

Gasping, Deuce said honestly, "I think I'd rather take a beating."

Don Rio shrugged. "Well, the day is young," he said.

Deuce's mouth hung open. Don Rio wasn't serious. *Was* he?

"Now, on to the business at hand," Don Rio said briskly. "Besides my precious Dina, my most favorite thing on earth . . . is my little piggy."

The bodyguard lifted a pink piglet from a cage on the ground and handed it to Don Rio, who held it to his chest and smiled.

"Ah, senorita," he said with a giggle. "Senorita Maria Consuela Rosa Santa Margarita de la Guardia. You may call her Pinkie. Two thousand dollars worth of cute." He gave Deuce a serious look. "I want you to take her into your care." He handed the piglet to Deuce, who took her gingerly.

"Here are my instructions," said Don Rio. He clapped his hands twice and one of the bodyguards gave Deuce a thick binder filled with directions for Pinkie's care.

"Do not let her out of your sight," Don Rio warned. "Return her to me safely in three days time, and I will give you my blessing."

"Hey, you won't regret this, Don Rio," Deuce said earnestly. "I—"

"Again, more about Deuce," Don Rio said impatiently. "Be gone."

He clapped his hands again. The bodyguards picked up Deuce's chair and carried him a short distance away, where they set him down on the sidewalk.

"You got Pinkie!" Dina exclaimed, her dark eyes glowing. "That's such a good sign."

"Yeah," Deuce said. "I have another reason why I dig you."

"What's that?" she asked.

"Your family might be crazier than mine," he answered.

Dina nodded. She couldn't argue with that!

CHAPTER 5

AS THE LITTLE CUTIE Queen dance rehearsals continued, CeCe and Rocky had been paying extra-special attention to Eileen, hoping that they could get her to coordinate her steps to the beat—or at least do them in the right order!

"Much better, Eileen," Rocky said, giving her a high five as the dance ended.

CeCe smiled at the little girl and gave her a fist bump. Then, as Eileen walked off, she frowned.

CeCe was having a tough time getting Eileen to follow the routine.

Rocky had to agree with CeCe. She really liked Eileen, but she had to admit it—the little tomboy just wasn't a good dancer!

While the contestants took a break, Sally marched over and said in a sweet voice, "CeCe? Rocky?"

"Yes, Sally?" CeCe asked.

"The other girls and I can't stand Eileen, and we want your help to get her out of the contest," Sally told her.

"Why?" Rocky asked. "Are you afraid that she's going to steal the crown away from you?"

"No, she's just not pageant people," Sally explained. "She has knobby knees and bad hair, and she talks about sports and dresses like a boy."

"Who are you, Little Miss Perfect?" Rocky asked. How did this little girl get to be such a pint-sized diva?

"Okay," Rocky said to Sally, "Eileen isn't the classic beauty-contest type, but she's real, and fun, and cute, and she has just as much right to be here as you do."

"Fine," Sally replied. She narrowed her eyes. "Trust me, this *will* end in tears." She whirled around and stomped back to the other girls.

Rocky watched her go in disbelief and then turned to CeCe. "What does she do for the talent part?" she asked. "Go out there and bite the heads off live chickens?"

"Those girls are terrible, mean, awful," CeCe said, shaking her head. "Just mean little girls."

Rocky looked at her. "You want to quit?"

"Oh, no, not now, baby," CeCe said, her eyes glinting. "Now I want to win!"

"Me, too!" Rocky exclaimed.

They turned to look for Eileen and spotted her sitting in front of the makeup mirror.

"Oh, Eileen," they said together in singsongy voices.

Eileen turned to face them. "Look, I did my own makeup," she said proudly.

Rocky and CeCe gasped. Eileen had drawn new eyebrows that stretched across her forehead. She had coated her eyelids with bright green eye shadow and smeared lipstick over not just her mouth, but her chin and cheeks as well.

"Did you save some for anyone else?" Rocky asked.

♪ ♪ ♪

A little while later, CeCe and Rocky were deep into their new project: teaching Eileen how to be a winning beauty queen. It was turning out to be a *lot* harder than they expected. They had all gone to CeCe's apartment in order to train in private.

"Now the most important ingredient in all pageantry is a winning smile," CeCe said. "Like this."

She put a hand on her hip, tilted her head, and gave an imaginary audience a huge, bright smile. Even though Rocky disapproved of pageants in principle, she had a bigger cause to fight for now—helping Eileen win! So she mimicked CeCe, adding a sassy wink to her winning smile.

"Now let's see yours," CeCe said to Eileen.

Eileen mimicked what CeCe had just done, but her smile came out more like a hideous clown grimace.

"Yowza," CeCe said, shocked.

Eileen sighed. "Why are you guys helping me?" she asked.

"Well, she's living out her fantasies through you, and *I'm* using you to make a feminist statement about how shallow beauty pageants are," Rocky explained.

"Could you say that in American?" Eileen asked.

CeCe grinned at Rocky and held her hand over her heart. "Oh, man, I love this girl," she said.

Rocky did her best to ignore this. Instead, she pushed the coffee table out of the way and said, "Okay. Let's start working on our slow spin."

CeCe took her place in the center of the floor, ready to begin.

"Now watch how she turns around without ever taking her eyes off the judges," Rocky said.

CeCe walked across the room, doing a very calculated spin. As she did so, she kept her eyes on the imaginary judges and gave a perfect wave.

Rocky grinned. "Okay, Eileen, it's your turn."

CeCe held up her hand like a traffic cop

signaling a stop. "Not done!" she barked.

She did one last turn and one last wave, then looked at Eileen.

"Chew on that, shortstop," she said with satisfaction.

Eileen rolled her eyes. Then she began stomping around the room. "Oh, look, I'm so pretty," she said sarcastically. "I can walk slow and turn in circles. Ooh!"

Rocky sighed. "Okay, new approach. Look, Eileen, I know this all seems sort of dumb–" she began to say.

"Important," CeCe interjected.

"And you probably feel a little silly–" Rocky continued.

"Beautiful," CeCe corrected her.

"But don't you want to prove something to those pageant people?" Rocky asked, giving Eileen a hopeful look.

"Like make Sally cry?" CeCe said.

"All right, fine," Eileen replied. "But you have to buy me a new baseball mitt."

"Done," Rocky said.

Eileen grinned. Then, smiling, she walked across the room and did a turn—all while performing a perfect wave!

"Yeah!" CeCe cheered, giving Eileen a gleeful high five. All of their hard work was starting to pay off. Maybe there was hope for Eileen winning the pageant after all!

CHAPTER 6

DEUCE WAS SERIOUS about winning over Dina, and that meant he had to be serious about taking care of Pinkie the piglet. He lay on his stomach next to the pig's cage, studying the binder that Dina's father had given him.

"'Thursday afternoon snack,'" Deuce read out loud. "'Brussels sprouts, potato peels, coffee grounds, and a dollop of mayonnaise'. Okay," he said reluctantly, closing the binder.

"Come on, Pinkie, eat something!" He nudged the bowl of food toward the piglet.

Pinkie stared back at him and didn't even take a nibble.

Deuce held the bowl up to his mouth. "Look at me, I'm a little piggy eating my little piggy snack," he said coaxingly. He took a bite. "Wow, that's surprisingly tasty."

As Dina walked up, Deuce had his face in the bowl, eating a little more.

"Deuce, slow down, you're eating like a pig," she said.

"And I'm loving it!" he exclaimed.

She put her hands over her heart and gave him a loving look. "Wow, you really *do* dig me," she said.

"I'm freaking out, Dina," he admitted. "I didn't sleep all night. Our whole future depends on that walking bag of bacon bits." He pointed dramatically at Pinkie.

"So let me take her for one night," Dina suggested.

Deuce was tempted, but he shook his head. "I can't," he said. "Your dad said the pig was my–"

"Relax, he'll never know," Dina said. "I'll take care of everything."

"Thanks, Dina," Deuce said, relieved. He picked up Pinkie's bowl and held it out to Dina. "Hey, do you think your mom can make this into a burrito for me?"

♪ ♪ ♪

The moment had finally arrived! It was time for the Little Cutie Queen contest. CeCe was so excited and nervous that she could barely speak! She did one last inspection of Eileen, who was dressed in a sparkly turquoise gown. Her curly hair flowed over her shoulders and her makeup was flawless. CeCe smiled excitedly. Maybe there was a chance Eileen could win—and get that new baseball mitt she was promised!

"There. You're perfect," CeCe said happily. "I know you're going to be the winner, CeCe."

Eileen turned to give her a questioning look.

"Oh, did I say *CeCe*?" CeCe laughed slightly. "I meant *Eileen*."

Meanwhile, Rocky was pacing next to them. She was so nervous! "Okay, we covered a lot of ground in the past few days," she said. "So, tell us what we learned."

Eileen pulled out a note card and began reading from it as Rocky mouthed the words along with her.

"'That pageantry is a farce imposed upon us by a society with outdated notions of femininity,'" Eileen read.

CeCe sighed and rolled her eyes.

"Except for . . ." Rocky prompted Eileen.

"'My mother, who had misguided but

well-meaning intentions,'" Eileen dutifully said, reading directly from the card.

CeCe caught Rocky's eye and frowned.

"What?" Rocky said defensively.

CeCe took a deep breath. If the pageant didn't start soon, she was afraid she was going to lose her cool!

CHAPTER 7

DEUCE WAS PACING anxiously on the sidewalk by the Italian bakery. It was time to give Pinkie back to Dina's father, but Dina— and more important, Pinkie—was nowhere to be found!

Suddenly, Dina came running up to him. Unfortunately, she didn't seem to be holding a small, beloved, two thousand dollar pig. . . .

"Where's Pinkie?" he asked, fearing the worst.

Dina looked upset. "Deuce, I don't know how to say this, but I-I-I—" she began. "I lost her," she finally admitted.

"You lost Senorita Maria Consuela Rosa Santa Margarita de la Guardia?" Deuce asked, aghast.

"Her skin looked a little dry, so I moisturized her," Dina said tearfully. "Then when I took her for a walk, she slipped out of her collar, and you know how hard it is to catch a greased pig."

"Oh, no, Dina, you've doomed us," Deuce moaned. "Not only are we not going to be Deuce and Dina, now it's going to be Dina and whatever-happened-to-Deuce-who-nobody-ever-heard-from-again!"

"We'll just tell my dad I lost her," Dina said. "At least he'll be mad at *me*, not you."

Deuce gulped. The idea of Don Rio being mad at anybody was too scary to think about for long!

He took a deep breath and then walked over to where Dina's father was sitting at his favorite sidewalk table—with Dina following. Don Rio's bodyguards stood directly behind him, as silent, unsmiling, and immovable as two small mountains.

"Ah, Senor Martinez," Don Rio said, smiling at Deuce and taking off his sunglasses. "Did you get the cologne I sent you?"

"Uh, yes," Deuce said nervously. "Thank you."

"Ah, come let me smell you." Don Rio stood and sniffed. "Ah! Now you smell like a man angel! But you know what I do *not* smell? Two thousand dollars worth of treasured family pet." He held up his little finger and frowned at Deuce. "Where is my Pinkie?"

Deuce bit his lip, but he knew he had to tell the truth. "Pinkie is . . . gone," he admitted. "You entrusted me with your treasure, and I failed you, sir. I'm sorry."

"I see," Don Rio said slowly. Then he clapped his hands.

The bodyguards each grabbed one of Deuce's

arms and pushed him down into a chair.

"Let me ask you a question," said Don Rio in a threatening voice. "Did you give Pinkie to anyone? Even for a *momentito*?"

Deuce glanced at Dina. She gave him a worried look in return.

He took a deep breath.

"No, sir," he said. "It was a hundred percent my fault."

The bodyguards moved in. They grabbed his arms again and lifted him in the air.

"Don't kill me," Deuce said quickly, his voice high-pitched from fear.

The bodyguards set him on his feet.

"Kill you?" Don Rio said roughly. He stood up and took a step toward Deuce until he towered over him. "I'm not going to kill you. I'm going to"—he grabbed Deuce's shoulders, then broke into a huge smile—"*kiss* you!"

He planted a kiss on one of Deuce's cheeks,

then the other. "You have passed my test," Don Rio said.

"But," Deuce stammered, "Pinkie's gone."

Dina smiled. "No, Deuce, Pinkie's right here," she said as one of the bodyguards pulled the piglet from a black case sitting under the table.

"You found her?" Deuce was totally confused!

"I never *lost* her," Dina said, carrying Pinkie over to her father.

Don Rio put his arms around Dina. "You could have sold out my Dina, but instead you took all the responsibility for yourself," he explained. "*Muy macho.*"

"You lied like a dog to protect me!" Dina exclaimed, beaming at Deuce. "Good lying is respected in my family."

"So this was a con?" Deuce asked, his voice rising. "You put me through all this and it was just one big con?"

Dina bit her lip. She hadn't expected Deuce

to be angry! Surely he knew this was just what her family did—didn't he? "Sorry?" she offered weakly.

"Sorry?" Deuce grinned at Dina as he took Pinkie from her arms. "It was beautiful! You played me like a stooge, yanked my chain, and drove me to Suckertown. I love this family!"

Don Rio laughed and clapped his hands. "Welcome, Deuce! Now, let me take you to lunch. Where do you want to go?"

Deuce petted Pinkie thoughtfully. "I don't know why," he said, "but I'm thinking barbecue!"

CHAPTER 8

THE CONTESTANTS IN THE Little Cutie Queen pageant were filled with excitement as they stood lined up across the stage. They had performed their dance and they had sung their song, and now the big moment had arrived! A new queen was about to be crowned. The little girls were so nervous they could hardly stand still.

And they weren't the only ones. The audience was filled with excited friends and family.

CeCe and Rocky clutched each other's arms and stared up at Eileen, wondering if they had done enough to help her win.

Gary's voice boomed out of the speakers. "And this year's Little Cutie Queen is . . ." He paused artfully, letting the feeling of anticipation flow through the room.

All the girls' faces were frozen with smiles, each contestant hoping that she would hear her own name.

". . . Eileen Keller!" Gary finally announced.

Eileen couldn't believe she had won! She squealed with excitement.

Gary smiled as he handed Eileen a huge bouquet of roses and put a sparkling crown on her head. The crowd applauded and cheered enthusiastically.

However, there was one person in conference room B of the Skokie Budget Inn who was not smiling, not clapping, and most definitely *not* happy.

"No!" Sally screamed. She fell to her knees in shock and pounded the floor with her fists. "I demand a recount!"

Rocky grinned at CeCe, as Gary picked up the little girl to carry her offstage.

"She was right," Rocky said with satisfaction. "It *did* end in tears."

"Put me down!" Sally shrieked as she was carried away. "That's not fair! I should've won! No!"

Meanwhile, Eileen had just finished taking her winner's walk. She marched to the edge of the stage and looked at the audience.

"Hey, yo! Stop your jibber-jabbering!" she shouted. "I got something to say."

Rocky grabbed CeCe's arm in her excitement. "All right, it's time for the truth bombs to drop. This is what makes it all worth it."

But then, instead of delivering the lecture that Rocky had written for her on all those cards,

Eileen smiled giddily and said, "This pageant is the *best* thing that's ever happened to me! I feel so pretty and special!"

CeCe widened her eyes in surprise. She smiled and started clapping. *That's my girl, Eileen!* she wanted to say. *Now you know how it feels to win!*

Rocky's face fell. "No, no, no, no!" she cried, hoping that Eileen could hear her. "Beauty comes from within. The cards, read the cards!"

Eileen ignored her. "I wish all little girls could feel as pretty as I do right now," she gushed.

"That little diva just sold us out," Rocky said in disbelief.

CeCe jumped to her feet. "Work it, CeCe! Work it!" Several mothers turned to look at her, frowning slightly.

CeCe caught herself. "I meant *Eileen*," she said weakly. Then she quickly sat down again.

Well, *that* was awkward, she thought. On the

other hand, sometimes it was hard to resist the beauty pageant spirit!

♪ ♪ ♪

The pageant was now over. All the contestants and their families had gone, leaving only a bare stage scattered with rose petals.

Then a voice from backstage said, "And the winner of the 2005 Little Cutie Queen pageant is . . . CeCe Jones!"

CeCe burst through the gold curtains and twirled across the stage. She was wearing a pink Little Cutie Queen sash and a huge smile.

Then she caught sight of the rhinestone crown sitting on the presenter's podium. She put it on her head and then knelt to pick up a couple of long-stemmed roses. "Ah! This is such an honor. Thank you so much. I love you all."

She was enjoying herself so much that she didn't hear Rocky come onto the stage.

"CeCe, let's go," Rocky said sternly. "It's enough already."

"Not now!" CeCe said through gritted teeth, her eyes still focused on the pretend audience. "I'm doing my glamour walk."

"But your mom's waiting outside," Rocky insisted. "Let's *go*."

"Fine," CeCe said, disappointed. She put the crown on a table, let the sash drop to the floor, pushed her way through the curtains, and headed backstage.

Rocky was right behind her until she got to the curtains. Then she stopped, turned around, and took another look at the crown.

She glanced around to make sure no one was watching. She giggled, then put the crown on her head and ran to the center of the stage.

"Thank you! Thank you, all!" she announced to the empty rows of seats. "This is the happiest moment of my life!"

"Aha!" CeCe bounded triumphantly back onstage. "Busted!"

Shocked, Rocky stopped smiling and put her hands on the crown, as if wondering what it was doing on her head. "Whoa, how did that get up there?" she asked innocently. She took the crown off, put it back on the table, and ran offstage.

Smiling, CeCe watched her go. When it came right down to it, no one could resist the beauty pageant spirit—not even Rocky!

THE BEAT GOES ON!

LOOK FOR THE NEXT BOOK
IN DISNEY'S
SHAKE IT UP SERIES!

STEP BY STEP

Adapted by N.B. Grace

Based on the series created by Chris Thompson

Part One is based on the episode, "Shake It Up, Up, & Away: Part 1," written by Rob Lotterstein

Part Two is based on the episode, "Shake It Up, Up, & Away: Part 2," written by Eileen Conn

CHAPTER 1

THE *SHAKE IT UP, CHICAGO* soundstage was buzzing as dancers got ready for the live show, which was just about to start. Some performers, dressed in black unitards decorated with pieces of red, purple, yellow, and green material, gathered near the stage. Others peered into makeup mirrors, checking their faces, which were painted with colorful stripes and zigzags. And everybody's heart was beating a little faster as the beginning of the show got closer and closer.

At that moment, Gary Wilde, the show's host, raised his hand to get the dancers' attention.

"Everyone who's participating in the *Shake It Up Cares* trip to Alabama to clean up the wetlands, the bus leaves from here tomorrow morning at seven!" he announced.

CeCe Jones, one of the show's background dancers, sighed. Last month, it had seemed like a great idea to sign up for the trip. They got to go on a road trip, help the environment, and maybe sign a few autographs for adoring fans. What could be better?

But now the reality was settling in—and it was not a reality that she liked.

"*Seven?*" she complained. "If *Shake It Up* really cared, they'd let us sleep in and pick us up at ten."

Her best friend, Rocky Blue, nodded in agreement. Rocky and CeCe both loved to dance, loved to perform, and loved to be onstage—what they definitely did *not* love was getting up early!

Gunther Hessenheffer, an exchange student from Germany and another background dancer on the show, saw this as his opportunity to make an impression on the show's host.

"Tinka and I will be there, Gary!" he said eagerly, glancing at his twin sister.

Tinka grinned and nodded. After all, she and her brother were all about glamour and pizzazz— not to mention lots and lots of sequins. They had more style than anyone else who danced on *Shake It Up*. She could just imagine how stunned the local people would be when she and her brother crossed the state line into Alabama!

But Gary didn't respond. The *Shake It Up* countdown clock had almost reached zero. They were about to go live!

"We're on in thirty seconds, people!" Gary shouted.

As the dancers scurried into position, Rocky

smiled. How cool are we? Cleaning the environment, making a difference. She beamed at the thought. After all, being a celebrity was great, but it was even better to use their fame to help other people.

At that moment, CeCe's phone chirped, the signal that she had a text message to read. As she glanced at the screen, her eyes widened with excitement.

"Ooh, breaking dance news!" she exclaimed. "They're holding open auditions this weekend for a new reality show called *Really? You Call That Dancing?*"

Rocky's face brightened at this news. "Hey," she said, "we should *totally* audition for that!"

In an instant, Rocky could see their future. She and CeCe would audition; they would be selected to compete; everyone in America would fall in love with them; they would win (of course); and, just like that, they would be stars!

As if she knew exactly what Rocky was thinking, CeCe smiled back at her. "Yes! Thank you," she said with relief. "I am so happy I didn't have to trick or manipulate you into doing this. So, while our parents think we're in Alabama, we'll just sneak off to L.A."

Rocky's smile vanished. "It's in L.A.?"

"Did I not mention that?" CeCe asked innocently.

Her friend gave her a warning look. "No!" Rocky yelled. "We are *not* sneaking off to L.A."

CeCe glared at her, then blew a raspberry in Rocky's direction. Sometimes, CeCe thought, it was a real pain to have a friend whose first impulse was always to do the right thing!

Before they could argue about it, however, they heard Gary's voice floating down from his usual spot on the catwalk high above the stage.

"Welcome back to *Shake It Up, Chicago,* where we're about to *glow* your mind," he said.

Instantly, all the lights went out. Despite the darkness, the audience could still see the dancers, thanks to the pieces of colored material sewn to their costumes. Each dancer glowed in the dark!

CeCe, Rocky, and the other dancers started their routine. As the music thumped, the glowing slashes of red, purple, yellow, and green wiggled and bounced across the stage. The audience cheered and clapped along enthusiastically.

But even as CeCe went through the moves she had practiced so often, she was only thinking of one thing: how could she get Rocky to let go of her inhibitions and head with her to Los Angeles—where superstardom surely waited for them?